Also by Tony M. Smith:

Bankers and Peasants

Tony M. Smith (author)

SmithTonyM@gmail.com

Instagram: @tony.m.smith

TheBookGiants.com

Cover designed by Ferdi Ka

The Book Giants

Los Angeles, California,

United States of America

The Sinful Nature of Sheep,

A Novella

Copyright 2021

The Book Giants

First published 2015

This 2021 SECOND EDITION published in the United States of America by

Tony M. Smith *&* **The Book Giants**

ISBN: 9780692720387

Dedicated to my
Grandad & Grandma.

ALL *the names,*
characters, and
incidents portrayed in
this story are
completely **fictitious**.

The Sinful Nature of Sheep

(SECOND EDITION)

A Novella

Tony M. Smith

"For a long time I
could not conceive how
one man could go forth
to murder his fellow,
or even why there were
laws and governments;
but when I heard
details of vice and
bloodshed, my wonder
ceased."

-Mary Shelley

CHAPTER ONE

Friday night.

I remember walking into Rose's Liquor Store with a gun tucked into the back of my jeans.

There was a girl behind the counter. She was cute, in a mean sort of way.

I took one step forward and pointed the gun at her face.

She didn't look scared at all and a brief moment passed before she asked,

"Is this a fucking joke?"

"The money! Now!"

She rolled her eyes, slowly removed the cash from the register, and then threw it on the counter.

After returning to my apartment, Philly and I counted the money, and we split it down the middle.

We spent the rest of the night smoking blunts and listening to Calcutta's *The Southbay Sleep Experiment*.

CHAPTER TWO

Saturday morning.

I turned on the news and searched through the apartment for Phil, but he was gone.

I lit a cigarette.

$900 was stacked on the table. I smiled. It was all I needed to publish my first book.

An attractive reporter in a red skirt didn't mention the liquor store robbery at all from the night before.

She only talked about a school bombing that was far far away from South Los Angeles.

I called Phil, but there was no answer.

I put on a jacket and once outside, I saw a Benz parked across the street.

The driver's window descended.

A fat man stuck his head out. "Get in."

I stood there until he set a gun on the dashboard.

I opened the passenger door and climbed in.

The man asked, "Sam?"

"Yeah."

"I'm Louie. Louie Acosi. Who do

you work for?"

Me: "I work at Movies N'
You."

"Yeah, the video rental
store." He smiled. "You got balls,
kid. Let me be the first to say
it."

Silence.

"Last night. That was you?"
He looked at me. "A guy named
Philly was the driver, yeah?"

"No. I never heard of him."

He smiled. "The liquor store
you guys robbed? It was ours."

"I don't know what you're..."

As he drove, the rosary
hanging from the rearview mirror
swayed along with the motion of
the car.

Louie interrupted me. "Take
this." He handed me an envelope.
"You got sent for. So just show up
and everything will be okay. Got
it?"

The car stopped in front of
my apartment.

I exited and he said,

"Don't be late, kid. And
bring that driver with you."

I was inside of my apartment
when I opened the envelope. The

letter inside had been typed in
red ink.

Morello's Italian Cuisine.
8 p.m.

CHAPTER THREE

7:30pm.

In cursive, written above the front door: Morello's Italian Cuisine.

There were at least eight guys in front of the place, and I overheard one of them say,

"Yeah, that's him."

Before my foot touched the first step, a man stopped me. A cooking apron was tied across his belly. He looked mean as hell.

He pointed at me. "Sam?"

"Yeah."

"Where's the other guy? The driver?"

"I don't know."

"No? Go in and sit down. And don't touch nothing."

I found myself in a very large dining room; red candles on the tables.

Louie Acosi stepped from behind two swinging metal doors with a massive bowl of pasta in his hand and a napkin folded inside his collar. I noticed how the tomato sauce on the corner of his mouth traced the smile on his face. He looked at his watch.

"Where's your friend?"

I shrugged.

"Okay. Come with me then."

I followed him through a hallway until we reached an unmarked door.

Louie's massive hands knocked twice and then gestured for me to enter. When I didn't go, he opened the door and ushered me in.

I remember how smoky the room was.

Five men were standing around this old man who sat at a black table eating pasta.

Louie turned around and exited, closing the door behind him.

Complete silence enveloped the room. I was out of place and I knew it.

The elderly guy looked up from his meal and stared at me. He finally waved me towards him, and he motioned for me to sit down next to him.

He pointed at his plate of pasta. "Hungry?"

"No, sir. Thank you."

"Careful. Politeness only works on sheep. I do not think you are fully aware of the trouble you have gotten yourself into, Sam Harper. You robbed me less than twenty-four hours ago. And now, here you sit. Where you'll be in the next twenty-four hours will be up to you. You robbed my liquor store. You and your friend."

"Yes."

"Where is my money, Sam?"

One of the guys standing behind the old man unzipped his jacket and took out a gun. He held it loosely in his left hand; pointing it at the floor.

"I'll get your money back," I said. "I promise."

"I want to know where your friend is. The driver. He needs to answer for helping you rob me. Where is he?"

"I don't know."

Mr. Morello looked at the five individuals standing behind him.

"Go find him."

Once they were gone, I caught a glimpse of an old oil painting hanging on the wall. It looked like it belonged in a museum.

"I'm Vincent Morello," The old man said. "And I've never seen you before. So why did you rob my store, Sam Harper? And why did your friend use his mother's car to drive you?"

"It's not my friend's fault. I swear. Don't blame him. He was just trying to help me because I needed the money to publish my first book. It was a mistake. I'm sorry. I just figured that if I got enough money, I could…"

"You're a writer?"

"Yeah."

"What kind of a writer?"

"Fiction."

"And what's your book about?"

"I can't tell you."

Silence.

"Sam, I asked you a question."

"I can't tell you, sir."

"How much money could it cost to publish a book?"

"A lot. The cover costs money and the formatting and the…"

How old are you?"

"17."

"A mere child. Yet, a child who robs liquor stores is no child at all. I should cut your hands off and kill you for stealing from me. I should even kill your family too."

"I don't have a family."

"No?"

"My grandmother raised me. She passed last year."

"Let me tell you a story, Sam Harper. Long time ago, there was a guy who ran Los Angeles. He had this illegal gambling spot. One night, when I was about your age, I walked in there and put a gun to the boss' head and demanded a job. You know what happened?"

I shook my head.

"Well, after the boss and his crew stopped laughing at me, he told me that if I ever pulled a gun on him again, he'd skin me alive. And then, he gave me a job. I worked my way up the ranks and that's how I got here. I had no family. Nobody. Look at me now. Now *I* run the whole city. I know how it feels to be alone. I know how it feels to want something, Sam Harper. Some people will starve without ever doing anything about it. They will die with their stomachs empty because they didn't want to live in the first place. But you do, Sam Harper. You do.

Even though we look different, I was you long ago. And when I was young, someone helped me. So now, I'm going to help you. Sound good?"

"I don't know if I…"

"You work at a video rental store called Movies N' You. Yes?"

"Yes."

"Not anymore. You work for me now. And because I appreciate your willingness to work, I'm going to give you a job. And this job will have two purposes, Sam Harper. Number one: it will prevent me from killing you. Number two: it will give you a chance to learn things that I myself learned as a young man. Oh yeah, you couldn't have spent my money that fast. So, I want it back. How does this all sound to you?"

"I'm not sure if…"

"I imagine that a writer needs his fingers, right? Last person who took something from me, I had one of my guys take four fingers from him. My guys are prone to go overboard because I only asked for one finger. And, Sam. I will take the fingers from your writing hand."

There was a knock at the door and two men entered the office.

One of them was the guy in the cooking apron. The other one placed a new plate of pasta in front of Mr. Morello. He looked only slightly older than me, in his twenties. The sleeves of his shirt were rolled up to his elbows and his forearms were covered in black tattoos. His neck and Adams apple were also blasted with ink.

Mr. Morello introduced me. "This, is Sam Harper. He'll be working in the restaurant from now on."

Both men stared at me.

"No disrespect, boss. But, you sure about this?"

Silence.

The guy about my age smiled and stuck his hand out to introduce himself.

"I'm Rudy Nola. This is my dad Benny Nola."

His father refused to shake my hand.

Mr. Morello: "Rudy, give him a tour of the restaurant and then cut him loose."

"No problem. C'mon, kid."

I rose and before Rudy and I exited the office, Mr. Morello said,

"Sam. From here on out, no more crime for you. Understand? You're a dishwasher now."

I followed Rudy into the dining room. His father stayed behind with Mr. Morello and within five minutes Rudy had casually showed me the entire place.

We proceeded into the kitchen and he handed me a white apron and a white button dress shirt that fit me too perfectly.

"This is yours. You'll be here in the kitchen most of the time. I serve the food and you wash the dishes."

If my reaction was faster, I could have dodged the fist that connected to the left side of my jaw.

I fell to the floor and when my eyes refocused, Rudy Nola was standing over me grinning.

"That girl you pointed a gun at last night, that's my girlfriend."

I got up as fast as I could

and we stood face to face.

Rudy: "Just be happy you're not in the dirt right now."

"Thanks." I responded, holding my warmed face.

"Anytime." He smiled, shaking my hand. "You'll do fine here. Just follow my lead, got it?"

"Got it."

"Okay cool. Come back tomorrow morning. 6 a.m. Don't be late."

My first thought was to get the hell out of there as soon as possible, so I damn near jogged past the men still loitering in front of the restaurant. Louie was standing there eating spaghetti.

"Hey, Sam! I heard you got a job now."

"Yeah."

"Cheer up, kid. It could've been worse. I mean, Mr. Morello could've had us bury you."

A thick glob of tomato sauce slid from his fork and hit the sidewalk.

"All the years I've known Mr. Morello, he never let anybody get away with robbing him."

"I didn't get away with anything."

He smiled. "That's true."

"I have to go."

"Hold on."

He disappeared into the restaurant and the men stood there just looking at me without saying anything. Phlegm landed next to my sneakers just as Louie returned with car keys in his hand.

"I'll take you home," he tried to say with a mouth full of noodles.

He removed the napkin tucked inside of his shirt, wiped his mouth with it, and then tossed it at the guy that spit at me.

"The boss said Sam is not to be touched. That means, whoever touches him is getting shot in the face. That includes spitting at him too."

Louie led me down the side of the restaurant and into a parking lot in the back.

Climbing into the passenger seat of a new Mercedes was way better than catching the bus at 10 o' clock at night.

After Louie dropped me off, I walked into my apartment and called Phil.

No answer.

I wanted to run away but I didn't know where to go. I didn't know how much power Mr. Morello really had and I didn't want to find out.

As my mind raced, I somehow closed my eyes and fell asleep.

CHAPTER FOUR

Sunday.

It was 5:30am when I arrived at Morello's Italian Cuisine.

I knocked on the front door.

Nothing.

I put my face up to the windows, but everything was dark inside. *What the fuck?*

I went to the parking lot in back and knocked on the back door. Nobody answered.

And then it began raining.

Around 5:45a.m., a delivery truck appeared and honked twice.

The back door of the restaurant opened, and I immediately ran to it. Mr. Nola stood there in the same folded cooking apron, and he looked me up and down.

"Hey! I knocked on all the doors!"

Mr. Nola: "Didn't hear it. Knock harder next time."

"I'm standing out here in the rain, asshole!"

He pushed me away from the door and looked me directly in the eyes.

"What did you just call me?

The only reason you're here is because the boss says so. If it was up to me, I would've killed you and been done with the whole thing. You ever talk to me like that again, and I'll put a bullet right through your head. With, or without permission. Understand?"

Before I could respond, he ordered me to help the guys in the delivery truck.

I proceeded to the back of the truck and a man tossed me a ten-pound bag of fresh potatoes from the loading door. I dropped it and they went rolling and bouncing around onto the wet concrete. All of the guys laughed.

"Good job, new guy!" One of them yelled.

After I carried in the rest of the stuff, a big man named Smalls shook my hand. After yawning, he introduced the other delivery guys and then tossed me a big roll of paper towels.

"So, you're a new cook here or something?"

"I think I'm more like a janitor."

He laughed. "Ain't we all,

kid. Nice to meet you. What's your name?"

"I'm Sam."

"Harper. Oh yeah, I heard about you. You're the writer, right?"

"Yeah."

"Out of all the liquor stores in L.A., you rob the one the boss owns."

Smalls had a pale scar that traveled from his collar bone to just below his left ear. I looked around and noticed that the other delivery guys had similar scars on their necks as well while rainwater dripped from their clothes onto the kitchen floor.

Smalls: "Next delivery, fellas. Let's go. See you tomorrow, Sam."

They filed past me and just as the door closed, Benny entered the kitchen and yelled about the floor being wet.

After mopping, I met the rest of the kitchen staff: an old immigrant that everybody called Dimples.

He walked in the kitchen with this ancient cassette player radio in his right hand, and a newspaper folded underneath his left arm pit. After studying me for a second, he shrugged his shoulders, and then began speaking Italian.

I didn't know what the fuck he was talking about, but I nodded my head whenever I felt a sentence had ended.

He unpacked the boxes from the delivery and slowly opened each cupboard and cabinet showing me where everything went.

Awhile later, Benny Nola stormed back in. He told me that a customer lost an expensive ring and he ordered me to climb inside the wet smelly dumpster in the parking lot and look for it.

After twenty long minutes, he returned outside with a smile on his face.

"Find that ring yet?"

"No."

"Even if you did, you wouldn't return it. Now get out of there because it's time to clean the windows in front of the restaurant. Hey, when this is over, you can write a book about digging in trash cans, huh?"

The windows were completely clean before I was ordered to clean them. But, Ass Face continued to come to the front of the restaurant and smear his greasy fingers over the glass to check for dust.

A Range Rover pulled up and Rudy stepped out with two girls. They were protected from the rain by a large umbrella.

"Hey, Sam!" Rudy yelled, as he walked up.

He shook my hand and introduced me to the girl on his left with a smirk on his face.

"You know each other. Right?"

It was the girl behind the counter at the liquor store.

"I'm sorry about the other night. I didn't know..."

"Don't worry about it." She punched me in the chest. "I can't pronounce my full name, so just call me Aleska. This is my friend Maria."

The girl to Rudy's right pushed back the blue hood on her jacket and smiled. *Damn*. I had never seen a girl that gorgeous before.

Aleska: "This is the guy that stuck that gun in my face."

"I heard about you, Sam Harper."

I began searching my mind to its depths trying my hardest to find something interesting to say, but my brain seemed to be broken. All I could do was stand there and look at her like an idiot.

Rudy: "Uh oh, here comes the Grim Reaper."

I turned around and Benny Nola threw me his keys.

"Go wash my car. I don't like watermarks on it."

*****

After washing Benny's car, I returned to the warm kitchen where Dimples was pouring cooking oil into a big pan on the stove. There were no dishes to wash so I curiously strolled into the main dining area.

People were seated randomly around the restaurant. I sat at a table and looked around. Everyone either covered their mouths with bread while they talked or leaned in very close to the person they addressed. All I could hear clearly was faint music from Dimples' radio and forks hitting plates.

I noticed each chair was positioned to face the front door. Every once in a while, one of the patrons would peer across the room at me. They looked like they all worked for Mr. Morello. I assumed they could smell a threat from miles away, and I was not one. I was just a goldfish inside a shark's tank trying my hardest not to be seen.

Rudy moved from table to table and I realized that he was well liked; the diners shoved cash into his hands and softly slapped him on the face.

My eyes scanned to a separate table and there was Maria and Aleska staring at me. Before I could smile back at them, Rudy tapped me on the shoulder.

"Fall in love another day."

"I've never been in a restaurant this nice before."

He laughed, "Sure. That's exactly what you were thinking

about."

Rudy led me into the kitchen. He walked over to a large pot on the stove, lifted the top, and stuck his index finger into the boiling tomato sauce. Dimples picked up a newspaper, rolled it up tight, and slapped the back of Rudy's neck with it.

Rudy placed the lid back on the pot and looked at me.

"Words of advice? Try to keep your eyes off Maria. At least while people are around. That's Mr. Morello's only daughter."

"That's Mr. Morello's daughter?"

"Yeah, and he would cut your balls off if he found out what you were doing to her in your head. And the fucked up part about it is you'd still have to work here too. And then, everybody would be calling you No-Nuts-Sam."

We laughed.

"I hear you, man."

Mr. Nola kicked the door open. "What's the hold-up!?"

Rudy picked up as many plates as he could carry and rushed into the dining room.

"And why are you standing there looking stupid for?" Benny stared at all the dirty plates piling up in the sink. "You need me to tell you every single fucking thing that needs to be done around here?"

*****

There was a knock at the back door and Dimples opened it.

Four men in all black entered. In the center of them was Mr. Morello and they proceeded to the dining room after Mr. Morello hugged Dimples.

Benny came in and told me to wash Mr. Morello's car.

When I was finished, I walked back into the restaurant and retrieved the envelope filled with stolen money out of my backpack.

I walked down the hallway where the office was, and Louie was standing in front of the door eating.

"Sammy boy, what's going on?" He shoved a mouthful of pasta into his mouth.

"I'm giving Mr. Morello back

his money."

Louie knocked on the door and then opened it. There Mr. Morello sat while his guys stood around him.

"Boss. Sam's got something for you."

Louie continued eating as I entered, and all eyes were focused on me.

"Why don't you swallow the food you already have in your mouth before taking another bite, you fat fuck?" One of them asked Louie.

"Fuck off."

Everybody laughed except Mr. Morello, who kept a fixed gaze on me. He waved me over and I laid the envelope on the table. Mr. Morello opened it with a butter knife and fork as if he were cutting a tender piece of rare meat. He removed the cash with his hand and then placed the green bills on a clean decorative napkin.

He looked up at me and said,

"You'll never steal again. Do you understand?"

I nodded.

A glob of tomato sauce from Louie's plate dropped to the floor.

Mr. Morello shook his head and looked at me. "You say you robbed my store to publish your book. And how much do you need to publish your book?"

I pointed to the cash on the table.

He smiled. "Too bad."

"Yeah."

"How could publishing a book cost that much money, Sam Harper?"

"I have to get the cover designed. The formatting. I have to order proofs. It all costs money. Working at the movie store wasn't paying me enough."

He smiled. "So instead of saving, you robbed me. By the way, where is your friend?"

"I haven't seen him, Mr. Morello. I swear."

Silence.

"Well, he needs to settle his debt with me. It'd be better if he walked in here than my guys drag him in here. Do you understand?"

Benny Nola stormed into the room. "I-cannot-believe-what-I'm-seeing-right-now. All those frickin' dishes in the kitchen, and you're on a damned lunch date!?"

"I'm just…"

"Get back to work! NOW!"

I looked at Mr. Morello and he nodded. I rose and exited the room.

* * * * *

Sometime later, Benny ordered me to flip all the tables and scrub the bottoms.

When I was done, Rudy and I sat at one of the tables with two big plates of lasagna and a bottle of wine.

Dimples exited the kitchen with a rolled newspaper and swatted Rudy on the back of the head with it. He snatched his wine and returned to the kitchen.

That night, Rudy and I were the only two in the restaurant; smoking cigarettes in the kitchen.

"Hey, remember that one time you put a gun in my girlfriend's face?" He smiled at me.

"C'mon, man. I already said I was sorry about that."

"That was smart of you to give the boss his money back. I think he likes you. And he don't really like new people that much. Especially the ones who steal from him."

"Yeah. He told me."

"Boss says you're some kind of writer."

"Yeah."

"Like, so you write books and shit?"

"I want to."

"That's cool. You like working here or what?"

"I mean, it's my first day. I don't even know what I'm…"

"Just follow my lead and you'll be okay."

*****

I showed up early my second day at exactly 5:50 a.m.

Five minutes later, the delivery truck's headlights illuminated the dark parking lot.

Smalls slid from the driver seat, put both of his hands on my shoulders and said,

"Hey, kid! Good to see you're still around."

Benny Nola opened the back door to the restaurant, and yelled,

"Let's go! Hurry up! Get those boxes in here! NOW!"

After the delivery guys and I brought the food inside, they left, and Dimples and Rudy appeared.

Rudy took some wine from a case of fresh deliveries. He removed the cork and began drinking straight from the bottle.

Dimples noticed Rudy and swatted him in the side of the head with a newspaper, causing some of the wine to spill on the tile floor.

Rudy ran into the main dining area and Dimples and Benny followed him out.

While I mopped up the spilled wine, the door leading to the parking lot opened.

That was the first time I met Dominick Morello, the boss' son.

He stood in the doorway, calmly removed his shades, and asked,

"Who the fuck are you?"

"Oh. I'm Sam Harper."

"My name's Dominick." He stuck his hand out. "So you're the guy? The robber. What's a writer doing robbing liquor stores?"

Rudy entered. "What up, Dom? You meet Sam yet?"

"This is the guy that almost killed your future wife."

"Yep. That's him."

"How's the jaw?" Dominick asked me, smiling.

"I'm fine."

Dominick pulled a joint out of his jacket pocket. "You in, Sam?"

"Hell yeah he's in!" Rudy answered, pushing me towards the exit.

We stepped from the kitchen and the three of us climbed into Rudy's Benz. That was my first time smoking weed in a one-hundred-thousand-dollar car.

*****

That entire morning, Rudy and Dimples taught me how to make

baked ravioli, cheesy chicken spaghetti, and mushroom lasagna.

At some point, Benny entered and told me,

"Enough with the frickin' cooking lessons. Mr. Morello wants to see you."

I walked to the office and one of Mr. Morello's guys was standing guard. He saw me, knocked lightly on the door, and then opened it for me.

Only Mr. Morello sat inside smoking a cigarette. He pointed to a chair next to his and as soon as I sat, he began speaking.

"Before bed, I used to tell my son and daughter the story of the child who wore a red jacket in the woods who got ate by the wolf."

"Oh, you mean *Little Red Riding...*"

"The story is about a little girl who gets lost on her way to her grandmother's house. Sad, I know. She decided to take a short cut through the woods. But a wolf was there waiting. Sad, I know. The wolf ate the grandmother and the little girl too. Such a very sad story. Don't you agree, Sam?"

"Yes."

He leaned closer and asked, "But, do you blame the wolf?"

"The wolf?"

"You cannot blame the wolf, Sam. Wolves are wolves. And wolves eat the weakest of sheep. Their natures are rather vicious naturally. So then, how must sheep live in a world filled with wolves, Sam?"

I shook my head.

"The little girl with the red jacket should have thanked the wolf when she saw him. Then, she should have shot the wolf in the face. She should have cut the wolf's head off. She should have stripped the wolf of all its fur. She should have worn the fur over her shoulders so that all the other wolves know not to come anywhere near her."

There was complete silence in the room as Mr. Morello smoked his cigarette before he asked,

"Sam, do you understand that some sheep will not follow their weak natures of being prey to their predators? Would you call this a sin?"

I shook my head.

"I need you to do a favor for me. Yes? Go to a place called Sixth Street Dry Cleaning. Someone named Nicky will be waiting for you. He'll give you something. I need you to bring it to me. This is very important, do you understand?"

He reached into his pants pocket, retrieved a ring of keys, and slid them across the table to me.

"Sam, can you do me this favor?"

"I can, Mr. Morello. I will." I grabbed the keys and exited his office.

Inside the kitchen, I removed my apron and as I walked out, Rudy said,

"Just get the package from Sixth Street and come right back here, Sam."

* * * * *

In the parking lot, I pressed the unlock button on the car key, and a Range Rover's lights flickered twice. The interior smelled like new leather and lingering cigarette smoke.

Sixth Street Dry Cleaning sat in between a pet supply store and a tattoo shop. I parked and slid out.

I noticed a man sitting in a wooden rocking chair outside the dry-cleaning place. He was cutting the end from a long cigar and before the tobacco hit the pavement, he asked,

"Sam?"

"Yeah. Mr. Morello said to come here and…"

"I know, I know. I'm Nicky. Come with me."

He led me inside and into a back office. On the walls hung a bunch of signed black-and-white boxing photos.

Nicky sat behind the desk, lit his cigar, and asked,

"So, you were the one that robbed the boss, huh?"

I nodded.

"Heard you're a writer."

"Yeah."

"Well keep me out of your stories. We never met and you never been here. Got me?"

"No problem."

He opened a locked drawer, and I was given an unsealed rectangular envelope packed with hundred-dollar bills.

"Damn."

"Hey, kid. You know what to do with that right?"

"Yeah. I'm taking it back to…"

A telephone rang, and he pointed towards the front door and waved me out.

When I arrived back at Morello's Italian Cuisine, there were no cars in the parking lot.

I went to the back door of the restaurant, but it was locked.

"Hey! Dimples! It's Sam! Dimples! Rudy!"

Nothing.

The front doors were locked as well. I reached into my pocket and used the keys Mr. Morello gave me. I put one in and it opened.

In the warm dining room, all the lights were on, but there was no one there. The restaurant would usually be packed at that time of night, but I was only met with emptiness.

"Mr. Nola? Dimples? Rudy!?"

Silence.

I politely knocked on the office door. "Mr. Morello?"

I walked around the entire restaurant before taking a seat at a table. I decided to just wait.

After half an hour or so, the kitchen door swung open.

"Hey, Sam!"

I immediately rose from my seat, "Maria."

"You remember my name?"

"Of course. I mean…yeah. Where is everybody? Your dad told me to go do something earlier and when I came back, nobody's around."

"Oh. Did you check the basement at all?"

"The basement?"

"Let's sit," she offered. "You have something for my dad?"

"Yeah."

I handed over the thick envelope along with the keys and she tossed them into her purse.

With a grin on her face, she asked, "How do you like working for Benny in the kitchen?"

I shook my head. "That guy is mean as hell."

She laughed. "Dimples should

make up for it though."

"Yeah. He's cool. Rudy's cool too. So, Dominick's your brother?"

"The heir to all this." She rolled her eyes.

I smiled.

"How old are you?"

I answered quietly like a ghost would hear us from the next table.

"17."

"Me too!" she leaned across the table and hit me on the arm.

A sound came from the kitchen and she stood.

"I have to get back to school now."

"At night?"

"Yeah. I stay in the dorms at the university."

"You're already in college?"

"Early acceptance."

"Damn. Nice."

She advanced towards the front door and before exiting, she turned around to smile at me.

The fantasy that was beginning to form in my mind would certainly have got me killed, so I brushed it away quick.

I could hear muffled noises

coming from inside the kitchen, so I peeked through one of the small circular windows in the swinging door.

I clearly saw Mr. Morello, Louie, and two of Mr. Morello's henchmen named Salvatore and Carmine Corso.

Although I couldn't unglue my eyes from the scene, something was telling me not to enter that kitchen.

And then I noticed him. A man. He was on the floor. A bloody mess. I didn't recognize who it was, and the poor guy had tape over his mouth. Salvatore picked the unknown man up and struck him in the jaw. The force sent him flying into a boiler on the stove. Thick red tomato sauce flew into the air and landed on the floor and counters.

Mr. Morello closed his eyes and shook his head. He then turned and nodded his head at Louie.

Louie pulled a black handgun out and pointed it at the center of the helpless man's chest.

A sudden flash.

BOOM!

The man swayed slowly back and forth like a very tall palm tree and then dropped.

Louie squeezed the trigger once more.

Mr. Morello said something inaudible and exited the back door.

Murder looked way too easy.

Louie suddenly looked into the small window in the swinging door and my scared eyes met his calm ones. He shrugged and looked away.

Salvatore Corso picked up the lifeless body and swung it over his shoulder. As he descended into the basement, blood trailed behind him until I couldn't differentiate it from the spilled tomato paste.

As Carmine Corso mopped the floor, I remember watching Louie eat while pointing to sections for Carmine to clean.

I turned away and headed towards the front door as fast as I could. Before exiting, I overheard Louie Acosi and Carmine Corso laughing.

Once outside, I vomited all over my sneakers.

* * * * *

It was my third day on the job
and as soon as I entered the
restaurant, Benny Nola demanded
that I clean the roof. That meant
I had to scrape all of the dried
bird shit loose and then use a
high-pressured water hose.

Rudy would climb the ladder
every once in a while, pick up
pieces of roof gravel, and toss
them at passing cars on the
street.

"Extra points for cop cars,"
he'd say. He'd have to climb down
when his father walked outside to
see where he'd disappeared.

The night before continued
replaying in my mind like an
annoying song and all I could do
was scrub the roof and try to
forget those gunshots that had yet
to stop echoing.

To be honest, being as far
away from that kitchen was good
enough for me.

I heard the ladder creak, so I
went over to it assuming it might
be Rudy climbing up again. It
wasn't.

"Maria."

"Hey!"

I grabbed her hand while she climbed onto the roof. I'll never forget those eyes and how she stared up at me. I felt like I had a superpower.

"Heartbreaker," she called me.

She stood inches away from my face and I could only see my tinted reflection on the surface of her sunglasses.

"Hot?"

Maria reached up and wiped the sweat from my forehead with her bare hand and I took a step backwards.

"You're scared of me, huh?"

"Me? No."

"Most guys won't talk to me, let alone look at me more than twice. Because of my family."

"Well, I'm talking to you, right?"

Maria sighed and looked up. "I can't wait to get out of here."

"And go where?"

"As long as it's not here, I don't really give a shit. Never mind."

"I think I get it."

"Really?"

"You're like a princess stuck in a castle, not allowed to play outside the palace walls with the poor kids."

She rose suddenly and walked to the edge of the roof. I knew that I had gone too far. I crossed a line. I had no right to tell Mr. Morello's daughter that she was a princess.

I was a dead man.

Once she got to the ladder, she turned and asked,

"Are you hungry?"

"Starving. But I need to finish before Benny comes up here and starts yelling."

"C'mon, Sam. The roof's not going anywhere. You can finish this later."

We descended the ladder and I followed her into the restaurant. She chose a table and Dimples eyed the main dining area from the kitchen door. Maria smiled and waved at him before he nodded and disappeared.

"When you leave Los Angeles, I'll go with you." I said.

"And why would you want to go

with me?"

"I'm stuck in this castle just like you."

She laughed.

"Rudy told me you're a writer."

"Yeah."

"What does a writer need to stick-up liquor stores for?"

"I was trying to self-publish my first book. And that costs money."

"So, you got the money, but my dad took it back?"

"Yeah."

"Almost, Sam Harper." She smiled.

"Almost."

"What's your book about?"

"It's about a bank robbery. It's called *Bankers and Peasants*."

"Nice title. So, is robbing liquor stores your job or…?"

"No." I smiled. "I work at a movie store. Movies N' You. Well, I used to. Not anymore."

The double doors to the kitchen swung open and Dimples entered with two plates of food.

He set the plates down with a smirk on his face before returning to the kitchen.

As Maria took her last bite, Dimples walked out of the kitchen to collect our plates and returned with two glasses of wine.

"Our very first date," she said.

"I guess I'm not afraid of you then."

"No. Not yet."

We managed to talk for a while, and even though I had the constant reminder of what happened to that man in the kitchen, Maria became the reason I wanted to show up to work every day. If I needed to be killed to be convinced I didn't love her, I was willing to risk it.

CHAPTER FIVE

It all happened on a Friday night.

Maria and I exited this really fancy restaurant called Jindo's Dragon around 8pm. As soon as I started driving, Maria leaned over to kiss me but then looked in the rearview mirror and asked,

"Is that car following us?"

"Which one?"

"The BMW."

I smiled. "BMW's don't follow people."

"I swear this car is following us. Look."

"Where?"

"Behind us. The BMW."

I stopped at a red light and finally turned around in my seat to look out of the back window and there it was.

My first thought was that it was one of Mr. Morello's henchmen. If my assumption was correct, they'd make sure that Maria got home in one piece and I make it home in several.

The BMW slowly switched lanes and rested on my side of the Mercedes.

Silence.

I never wanted a light to turn green so bad in my entire life.

I just remember smiling at Maria before she pointed behind me and yelled,

"Sam!"

Whipping my head to the left, I saw the passenger door to the BMW open. A guy stepped out. His right hand was hidden inside of his jacket and as he moved towards us, out came a solid gold handgun.

I un-clicked my seatbelt, swiveled as fast as I could in the leather seat, and after unlocking the door, I kicked it open.

The force split the guy's face and he dropped.

The gun slid away as lighting flashed in the distance.

"Sam!" Maria grabbed my shirt. "Don't!"

I got out and slammed the door behind me.

Everything turned gray when I wrapped my fingers around that gold pistol.

When the other doors to the BMW opened, more people jumped out. They stood there for a minute before shooting at me.

When I shot back, I struck the guy behind the wheel because the BMW accelerated into a concrete light pole.

I looked behind me when I heard someone violently pulling the door handle on Maria's side of the car.

I fired through the back window of the Mercedes. The vibration shattered all the glass in the car. Maria screamed, removed her seatbelt, and squeezed into the small space below the dashboard.

I ran to her side of the car and a man was on his back holding his chest. Red bubbles formed around his mouth as he tried his hardest to inhale oxygen.

I shot him right in the face.

I turned back to the BMW and one of the guys was sliding a magazine into an assault rifle. I began firing at him and a bullet ricocheted off the asphalt and flew into his leg.

He dropped to the ground and then pointed the gun at me.

Nothing.

He struck the side of it with his fist and pointed it at me again.

Nothing.

I walked straight towards him. He threw his broken gun at my feet and yelled some racial epithet at me. I pointed the gold-plated pistol at him and let a round burn through his throat. He died clutching his neck.

On the other side of the BMW, the driver was dead while another held his head off the oil-soaked ground.

I emptied the 9mm into both of them.

Maria's car screeched to a stop next to me.

"Sam! We gotta go! Please!"

The sound of sirens wailed in every direction.

After I jumped into the Mercedes, Maria touched my entire body to make sure I wasn't leaking blood from some hole.

We sped away and my heart was beating so wild that I felt that it would leap from my chest at any moment.

We stopped in front of

Aleska's house at midnight. Maria slid from the car and her best friend held her as she cried.

Rudy calmly strolled to the Mercedes and asked, "Want some beef jerky? It's the teriyaki flavor."

I exited the car and he put his arm around my shoulders.

"Sam!" Maria yelled. "I love you." She said, hugging me tight.

"I love you too."

"Let's go for a ride," Rudy told me.

Before Rudy sped out of the driveway, he told Aleska to hide Maria's car in the garage.

CHAPTER SIX

Rudy Nola and I were alone in the dark parking lot behind Morello's Italian Cuisine. We were both leaning against the back of his Audi and he wanted to hear what happened in complete detail.

"I don't know what happened." I told him. "We went to dinner and..."

"Don't sweat it, Sam. You got Maria out of there. That's all that counts. And good thing that AK didn't work, or you'd be dead right now."

A chill ran down my spine.

"I could be dead right now." I whispered.

"Yep, you could be dead right now. Anyways, where is that golden gun?"

"It's in Maria's backseat."

"Sam, we're gonna share it. Me and you."

"You can have it, Rudy."

"Bet!"

A black Mercedes slowly entered the parking lot and stopped. The front headlights blinked at us.

"That's Louie. Let's go."

Rudy got in on the passenger side and I climbed in the back. Louie turned around in his seat and looked at me.

"You alright, kid?"

"Yeah." I nodded.

"You're alright."

"Let's get outta' here!" Rudy yelled.

*****

Rose's Liquor Store soon appeared.

Louie parked in the dark alley behind it. When he and Rudy exited the car, I just sat there wanting to disappear.

Rudy knocked on the window and I took a deep breath before getting out.

Louie unlocked the backdoor of the liquor store and I followed him in. Rudy locked the door behind us.

I was led down into a dark basement. Once we got to the bottom, Louie flicked an overhead light on.

I realized I was about to be shot dead. I wanted to grow old with Maria, so it saddened me to think that my last view would be of bleach containers in a liquor store basement.

"You fucked up, Sam." Louie said.

"I know I wasn't supposed to be with Maria but..."

"No. Not that," He shook his head and grinned.

"That's frickin' bad enough." Rudy threw in.

Louie: "Sam, you need to understand that you took the boss' only daughter into enemy territory tonight. That restaurant you and Maria went to is the enemy's main headquarters."

"Enemies?"

"Yeah, this other crew in L.A."

"It's been war for years."

"War?"

"Yeah. A war over control of the whole city."

"It all comes down to who controls the drugs, prostitution, guns, and even high-profile robberies."

"High-profile robberies?"

"Yep. Let's say you rob a bank

in L.A., you better get the approval from Mr. Morello first or…boom, you die."

"Mr. Morello is the boss of all bosses in Los Angeles."

"I swear I didn't know about any war or the other crew. I would've never taken Maria to…"

"You practically gave them a gift by taking Maria there." Louie said. "They probably spotted her soon as she entered the place. And all they had to do was wait patiently until you left."

"Hey. Don't feel bad about killing them. They would've killed you and sent pieces of Maria's fingers to Mr. Morello. That's how bad this war is."

"I know you saw me shoot that man in the kitchen." Louie added. "That was the other crew's messenger. He offered Mr. Morello a deal to split the city in half. The boss declined so I put a bullet in the messenger's face." Louie shrugged his shoulders as if he was talking about an event that happened decades ago. "No deal."

Rudy coughed, barely able to cover his amusement.

The basement door opened and closed causing the three of us to look up, and then I heard shoes calmly descending the wooden steps.

It was Maria's older brother. Dominick proceeded past Louie and Rudy with a gun in his hand. I mentally prepared myself to get shot. Mr. Morello's son removed his shades and said,

"You almost got my sister killed. That's unforgiveable, Sam. Sorry."

He raised the gun so that the barrel was staring at my forehead.

Silence.

"Hey, Dom." Rudy tried. "He didn't mean to do it. He didn't know. Sam's okay."

"Did you get the okay from your dad, Dominick?" Louie asked. "The boss says Sam's not to be touched. Remember?"

"No. No. No. Wrong," Dominick answered. "My dad gave Sam a pass for robbing the liquor store. He never said nothing about him almost getting my fucking sister killed. Sorry, Sam. You're cool, but I don't let nobody put my family in danger. Got it? Nothing personal. Any last words?"

I closed my eyes and responded, "Just tell Maria I love her, and I never meant to put her in danger. I'm sorry for…"

"Wait. You love my sister?"

I opened my eyes. "I do."

"And you're not just saying that because I got a gun pointed at your head, are you?"

"No. I really do love her. And I know..."

"First off, you don't know shit about shit. If you knew anything, you would've never taken Maria into enemy territory. You got her out of there which is good. But you killed four gangsters in the street tonight, Sam. So now, you got a *big big* problem."

"I do?"

Rudy: "You killed four known gangsters and left them in the middle of the street like dogs."

"You're probably green lit, Sammy boy."

"Green lit?"

Dominick: "They'll find you and they'll kill you."

I looked down at the floor of the basement. "Damn. What the fuck did I do?"

"You did what you had to do, kid" Louie said. "Don't worry, you're with us now."

"Yeah. You're with us now." Dominick added.

"But what about the cops?" I asked. "Won't they come looking for me?"

"You said you killed everybody there, right?"

I nodded.

"Then that's that. No witnesses equal no cops."

"And if they do come around, you're just a dishwasher. Remember?"

Louie moved to the corner of the basement and kicked aside an old rug that hid a door in the floor. He opened it and lifted out six black duffel bags.

"Alright. So, we got some automatics, some shotguns, some pistols, a shitload of bullets and…some other stuff."

With a big smile on his face, Rudy began digging through the bags.

"Look," Dominick began. "The next phase of this war will be waged by us. We're gonna take care of this shit ourselves. My dad knows nothing. Got it? I'm taking over this crew one day, so my name needs to strike fear in the street. Put the word out, Louie. Any motherfuckers that had anything to do with trying to hurt my sister or kill Sam, they're dead."

"You got it, Dom."

"Hell yeah." Rudy whispered.

CHAPTER SEVEN

Saturday morning.

Before I entered the backdoor of Morello's Italian Cuisine, my phone vibrated in my pocket.

Maria: "Sam, you saved my life last night."

"I should've stayed in the car."

"You were only trying to protect me. Are you going to leave town now?"

"What do you mean?"

"I just figured that you'd leave L.A. as fast as you could."

There was sadness in her voice.

"I'll never leave without you. We're leaving together. You and me."

Silence.

"I love you, Sam."

"I love you too and I'll see you later."

I entered the back door of the restaurant and the first person I saw was Mr. Morello. He was being followed by about 20 guys. My stomach sank.

"Sam."

"Yes, Mr. Morello."

"I'm leaving to New York. My son Dominick will be in charge in my absence. You'll follow what he says as law. Okay? Good."

He gently slapped my face and before exiting the restaurant, he said,

"So, you still won't tell me what your book is about, huh?"

"I can't, Mr. Morello."

He smiled and nodded at one of his henchmen. The guy then reached in his pocket and handed me a thick roll of cash.

Mr. Morello: "By the time I get back from New York, I want that book of yours published. You understand? Goodbye, Sam Harper."

And the old man faded out of the doorway with his twenty goons right behind him.

CHAPTER EIGHT

One night, after cleaning the entire restaurant, I finally turned the lights out and locked the door.

A loud engine revved twice, and I heard someone yell, "Yo, Sam!"

It was Rudy and he was behind the wheel of a brand-new Porsche.

"Get in and buckle the fuck up!"

He slammed his foot on the gas pedal and the rear tires spun into motion on the dry asphalt; the burning rubber kicked smoke into the night air.

"You like?" He asked.

"Hell yeah! Where'd you get this?"

"The docks. When a new shipment of exotic cars comes in, I get to pick what I want. The rest get sold and all the money goes to Mr. Morello."

"All of it?"

"Every last penny. He's the boss."

"So where are we going?"

"To a bonfire."

Rudy drove to the other side of L.A. and parked behind a Mercedes on a dark street. Dominick, Carmine, and Salvatore exited.

Dominick opened the trunk and removed a thick blanket covering six red gas containers. They all took one.

"Put on your ski-masks," he said. "That piece of shit strip club is around the corner. Let's go."

Across the street from Red Hours Strip Club, there was a man guarding the entrance with his arms folded.

Salvatore walked towards the bouncer alone. Once he was close to the guy, he grabbed a gun from his belt, and he hit the guy across the jaw with it. The man folded to the ground without a sound. Salvatore then dragged the unconscious bouncer around to the parking lot.

We walked over to the parking lot and Carmine set his gas cans down and kicked the trunk of a BMW open. Salvatore hauled the man inside and slammed the trunk shut.

I watched Rudy break all the windows of every single car in the parking lot. While the alarms sounded, Salvatore and Carmine poured gasoline inside.

"Watch me, Sam." Dominick said.

He removed a flare from the black bag I was holding, slid the top against the concrete, and flames began spraying out of it. He chucked the flare into a Mercedes and the interior ignited immediately.

"You love my sister, right?" He asked me.

I nodded.

"Then you'll throw these flares in all these cars."

"Okay."

"Me and Rudy are going in the front door. Sal and Carmine, you guys go to the emergency exit door in the back.

As soon as I began striking flares and tossing them into the cars, Salvatore rushed inside the strip club with Carmine following close behind. Dominick and Rudy stormed the front.

I stood there and watched

every car in the parking lot burn.

Sometime later, the backdoor opened, and Dominick stuck his head and looked at the melting cars.

"Good job." He pointed inside. "Come on."

I had never been in a strip club before. And so, I entered a dark place decorated with floor length mirrors that surrounded the entire interior. The scent of cigarettes, sweat, and perfume clung to the walls everywhere.

And then, I tripped on something.

I remember looking down and seeing dead people strewn about the floor.

Everyone had been brutally shot and killed.

The newspapers later called it the 'Red Hours Massacre.'

Carmine, Salvatore, and Rudy moved slowly through the club shooting anyone who may have still been alive.

"I wonder how all these people will explain themselves when they get to Heaven." Rudy said.

"What do you mean?" Carmine

asked, before putting a bullet into a shaking body.

BOOM!

Rudy: "I mean, this ain't a church. They all got killed in a dirty ass strip club. How do you explain that shit to the guy deciding if you get into Heaven or not?"

Carmine and Salvatore began laughing.

"Yeah! Sorry, God. I was staring at some tits and somebody shot me in the face."

They all laughed.

"Hey!" Dominick commanded. "We got shit to do! Let's get to work!"

The four of them then poured gasoline all over the floor and the bodies. Once the gas cans were emptied, Dominick placed a flare in my hand.

"For my sister."

I heard one of the cars explode in the parking lot outside.

"Let's burn this motherfucker down!" Rudy yelled.

We all struck our flares and tossed them until it felt like the entire world caught fire. And for days, I couldn't shake the scent of gasoline from my nose.

CHAPTER NINE

It was a Sunday morning when Rudy called me and said,

"I'm outside your building. Come down."

I slid out of bed and kissed Maria.

When I climbed into Rudy's Porsche, he slammed his foot on the gas pedal.

"Where are we going?"

"We're meeting Salvatore and Carmine."

In the alleyway in the back of Rose's Liquor Store, Rudy parked behind three black BMW's. The Corso brothers walked over to us and we all shook hands.

Rudy told Sal to take the BMW in front and Carmine would be in the middle. I was in the third car with Rudy.

"Jindo's?" Carmine asked.

"Yep," Rudy responded. "Let's go."

Within no time, Rudy had parked a block away from Jindo's Dragon Restaurant.

"This is the place me and Maria came to." I said. "The night we almost got killed. What are we doing here?"

"Just a little drive-by. Look, Salvatore will drive past the restaurant. He'll start shooting at it and that will make everybody inside drop to the ground, right? When they think the violence is all over, Carmine will drive past and shoot at the place again. Then us right after."

"Damn."

Rudy reached in the backseat and set on my lap an automatic shotgun.

"Damn? Some of those guys you killed the other night, have friends in that restaurant. You can either do something about them *now* or wait for them to do something about you *later*. I mean shit, they're probably in there right now planning on how to kidnap Maria again."

Rudy called Salvatore.

"Go."

All three BMWs advanced.

Sal sent seven wild rounds into the windows of Jindo's Dragon.

BOOM! BOOM! BOOM! BOOM! BOOM! BOOM! BOOM!

Halfway past the restaurant, Carmine Corso shot the place up next.

BOOM! BOOM! BOOM! BOOM! BOOM! BOOM! BOOM!

There was a silence until a handful of bloody people screamed as they began stumbling out of the restaurant.

Once our car stopped, Rudy yelled,

"Now!"

But I was stuck. I just sat there.

Rudy glared at me and shook his head.

He then snatched the shotgun from me, opened the driver side door, and walked around to the sidewalk.

And all those people. I watched him kill every single person.

After Rudy got back in, he left a trail of tire marks on the asphalt halfway down the street.

When we made it back to Rose's Liquor Store, the Corso brothers left as if it was business as usual. I began walking to the Porsche when Rudy pointed at the

BMW.

"Like the Beemer?"

"Of course. It's dope."

He tossed the key to me.

"Take it. It's yours."

"Thanks, Rudy. Damn."

"No problem. And hey, next time I give you a gun, you better shoot somebody. Meet me back at the restaurant."

He closed the door and sped out of the alley.

CHAPTER TEN

I was on my lunch break one day smoking a cigarette in the parking lot of Morello's Italian Cuisine. I noticed Rudy screaming into his phone. When he ended the conversation, he walked over to me and said,

"Let's go."

We arrived at the docks.

A cargo ship was on fire. The flames stretched to the sky and there was nothing but black smoke everywhere.

Rudy jumped out and I followed.

Burnt debris littered the dock and through my burning eyes, I saw a helicopter drop water onto the boat.

I ran over to Rudy.

"Fuck," he whispered.

In the distance, the silhouette of a heavy-set man jogged towards the two of us.

"Rudy! Rudy! I'm sorry!"

Rudy walked towards the screaming man.

"You're fuckin' sorry!? All you had to do was protect our

shipment when it washes into this pissy dock! That was your only job, Jimmy! We took you off that other thing because you fucked that up. Gave you another chance with the docks. All you had to do was keep your eyes open! And you can't even do that right!"

"It was a bomb, Rudy. It exploded as soon as the ship pulled in. All the cars are gone. I'm sorry."

"This was your last chance, Jimmy."

"It wasn't my fault!"

Rudy threw a right hook and connected with the left side of Jimmy's neck. He fell to the ground clasping his throat.

"Rudy...Rudy..."

"What the fuck do I pay you for!? To sit on your fat ass!? You stupid fuck! Do you know what was in the trunks of those cars!?"

He grabbed the guy around his blue collar and began punching him repeatedly in the center of the forehead until Jimmy stopped defending himself.

I remember the blood dripping from Rudy's swollen hand as he continued swinging. I tried to pull him off and he pushed me away.

"Go get the fuck in the car, Sam!"

He released Jimmy and savagely kicked him in the ribs over and over.

Rudy then advanced towards me.

"Sam, you ever do that again and I'll kill you. You don't see nothing. You don't hear nothing. You don't know shit, understand? So just stand out of the way and wait until somebody tells you to do something. Got it?"

Rudy sped without saying a word until we were in front of my building.

"Don't come to the restaurant tomorrow. I'll call when we need you."

As I walked into my apartment building and up the steps, I realized that I was no longer allowed in a place that frightened me.

I sat motionless on the couch staring at a complete stranger in the black mirror on the TV screen.

CHAPTER 11

Monday morning. I actually wanted to go to the restaurant, but I had been banished. I should have used the godsend to get the hell out of Los Angeles. But, love. It seemed to hold much more weight than logic. There was no way in hell I was leaving L.A. without Maria.

Knock. Knock. Knock.

Standing there smiling at me, was a rose that became prettier every time I saw her.

Maria kissed me as she entered.

I turned around, and the golden gun was pointing at my face.

She giggled and asked, "Want it?"

"Give it to me."

"Nope."

I walked towards her and she ran when I chased her throughout my apartment. She laughed even harder when I caught her.

"I have to take a shower."

"Smelly boy!" She threw a pillow at me.

*****

My horrible attempt at
breakfast made Maria smile. After
we ate, she began going through
all my stuff.

When she looked in my closet,
she found a million notebooks
filled with a million stories.

She grabbed some of them and
jumped on top of me in bed. She
wanted me to tell her about each
one. I had never told anyone about
my stories before. Philly and my
grandma were the only people who
had ever heard my stories.

"So, you really robbed my dad
to publish your first book?"

"Yeah. I finally finished
writing it. I was trying to get
published by a major book company.
But then, I got a million
rejections from literary agents.
So, I decided to self-publish on
my own. And that costs money, and
I didn't have any. So, my best
friend Phil, he came up with a
plan. We thought it'd be simple

enough to rob one of the million liquor stores in L.A. as long as nobody got hurt."

"And one of those million just so happened to belong to my dad."

"Yeah. I'm glad I did though. I met you."

She kissed me. "Sounds like a good love story."

CHAPTER 12

Rudy called me about a week or so later to return to work.

At the restaurant, Dimples opened the back door with a lit cigarette loosely dangling from his lips. He looked pleased to see me and after saying something in Italian, he flicked the cigarette outside and closed the door behind me.

Taking the initiative, I began cleaning all of the windows outside.

Mr. Nola arrived as I was finishing. He stopped the car and lowered the window.

"Sam."

"Good morning, Mr. Nola."

"Just who in the fuck told you that you could take a fucking vacation around here?"

"I...I'm..."

"Let me ask you another question. Were you with Rudy at the docks about a week back?"

I shook my head.

"You sure about that?"

"I wasn't with him."

"Okay. Did you mop the dining

room yet?"

"As soon as I'm done cleaning these windows, I'll…"

"Well get to it! And when you see that son of mine, you tell him I'm looking for him."

I was smoking a cigarette when Rudy's Porsche entered the lot. I removed the gold gun from the trunk of my BMW and walked over to him.

"Sammy!" He slid out of the Porsche.

I handed the gold nine-millimeter to him.

"This is it!? Hell yeah! Thanks, man!"

He pointed the gun towards the sky as if he was going to shoot a hole through a cloud.

"Nice."

He placed the gun underneath his driver's seat, and we entered the kitchen.

Mr. Nola stormed in and yelled,

"Rudy! Get the fuck over here! Now!"

Rudy walked over to his father.

"You out of your fucking

mind!? Who in the fuck told you to take Sam with you to the docks?"

"I didn't."

Dimples didn't look up at all but continued slicing tomatoes.

"Sam." Mr. Nola pointed at me. "You didn't see Rudy beat a man named Jimmy to death?"

"No. I didn't see anything."

"Good. You better keep it that way, dishwasher. Or, I'll just cut your tongue out."

Mr. Nola walked into the dining room.

As Rudy exited the back door, he looked at me and said,

"Let's go."

I climbed into the Porsche with my dirty apron still on and he sped out of the driveway.

"Remember that shipment of cars got destroyed at the docks?"

"Yeah."

"That's a lot of fucking money we lost, and I'm not gonna be the one to tell the boss we lost his money. Are you? So, it's up to us to make it right. Right?"

"Yeah. What do we have to do?"

Rudy parked and pointed out the window.

"You see that classic car dealership over there? Far East Imports?"

"Yeah."

"Well, that place belongs to our enemies. They got some of the rarest cars that ever touched the planet. And we're taking every single fucking car they got as payback for blowing up our shipment at the docks. Motherfuckers."

He punched the steering wheel with this huge smile on his face.

"We're doing this tonight?" I asked.

"No. Right now. It's 9:58. They open the place at 10am. Me and you will be their first customers of the day. You know those big trucks that carry new cars? I got my hands on one and it's around the corner. Carmine and Sal are waiting for my call. All the cars will go into the truck."

He reached in the backseat and gave me a ski mask.

"You ready?" He removed his shades and put on his ski mask.

I nodded.

"Sam, take that fucking cooking apron off. Let's go."

He retrieved the golden gun and a baseball bat from the trunk. He handed me a .45 and I stuck it in my pants.

I followed Rudy into the car dealership.

No one noticed us until he slammed the baseball bat on the main desk causing the man behind it to leap away from his computer.

"Watch them!" Rudy pointed the bat at two employees sitting on the opposite side of the room.

I removed my gun and pointed it at them.

The women threw their hands above their heads immediately.

"Keys!" Rudy screamed.

The man rose, knocking his manager sign from his desk. He led Rudy to a back office.

I walked steadily behind the two nervous women into the office.

The manager of Far East Imports began turning the dial of a safe.

Rudy turned the bat upside down and rammed the wooden handle into the man's skull.

"Hurry the fuck up!"

The women screamed.

A thin trail of blood raced down the man's forehead and into his eyes. The safe door finally popped open revealing stacks of cash and shiny car keys.

Rudy pointed towards the ladies crouched fearfully in a corner. The man moved as fast as he could. I noticed one of the ladies remove an elegant scarf from around her neck and press it on the manager's head.

After removing everything from the safe, he gave me some zip ties and thick electrical tape that he took from a desk drawer.

"On your stomachs!" Rudy yelled at the three hostages. "Hands behind your backs!"

All three employees laid face down on the floor and we zip tied their hands behind their backs and taped their mouths.

Rudy took out his phone and sent a text.

The Corso brothers walked in with ski masks covering their faces. Carmine tossed Rudy some empty black bags while Salvatore collected the car keys from the floor. After they exited, Rudy and I packed all cash into the black bags.

From the window, I watched Salvatore exit the huge truck and roll up the back cargo door revealing two car racks. It was perfect. Both brothers then carefully drove every car into the back of the truck until the parking lot was empty.

Rudy snatched the tape from the manager's mouth, kneeled down next to him, and asked,

"Where's the rest of the stuff?"

The man stuttered, "Stuff?"

Rudy stood and swung the bat into the guy's stomach.

"Don't play stupid with me, Mr. Manager. Where is the rest of the stuff?"

The manager stayed silent. Rudy seized a globe positioned on the desk and struck the man's head with it. The force left a dent in the world.

"Behind the painting! Behind the painting! In the wall!"

I glanced at the wall towards

the painting and then at Rudy. He nodded while gently spinning the blood-stained globe around its metal axis.

I gently lifted and placed the heavy framed oil painting on the floor revealing another safe.

"Numbers?" Rudy demanded.

After the Far East Imports manager told me the numbers, I entered them, and the metal door unlocked. Inside, cash was sitting comfortably on top of 15 large clear bags filled with white powder.

"Look for a janitor's closet." Rudy told me. "We're gonna need some more bags."

I exited the room and grabbed a box of black trash bags. And just before I returned to the back office I heard,

BOOM! BOOM! BOOM!

When I walked in, the three dealership employees were dead.

Rudy snatched the box out of my hand and began scooping all the safe's contents into as many bags as it took.

We exited Far East Imports carrying bags and bags filled with cocaine and money.

  After stuffing everything in his Porsche, Rudy went back into the dealership and retuned with the painting that hid the safe.

  "The boss will like this one."

CHAPTER THIRTEEN

I was inside the restaurant sweeping the dining area late one night. Everyone was gone except Mr. Nola who was at one of the tables counting money.

I heard tires screech outside. All of a sudden, the front door flew open and the owner of Sixth Street Dry Cleaning burst through bloodied and beaten. I immediately ran over to him after he collapsed on the floor.

"Mr. Nola!" I yelled.

Benny jogged over. "Nick!" He yelled. "What the fuck happened!?"

"Some masked motherfuckers ran into my shop. Started beating the shit out of me with wrenches! They-shot-me-in-the fucking-hand! And then they dropped me off here. Right in the fucking street like a dog!"

Mr. Nola hoisted Nicky up from the floor.

"Don't you worry, Nicky. Mr. Morello will make this right."

"They told me to tell Mr. Morello that we're all dead. All of us. They're coming for all of us. One by one." He looked at me.

"Even you, kid. They want you bad."

While carrying Nicky to the kitchen, Mr. Nola looked at me and said,

"Instead of standing there like a dumbass, clean that blood before it stains my floor."

I descended into the basement and once I returned to the dining room with cleaning spray and a hand brush, Dominick was staring at the dark red spot through his shades.

"Sam. What the fuck's going on around here?" He asked.

"It's Nicky's blood." I said, while scrubbing the floor. "He got shot in the hand and beat pretty bad. They left him in the street outside."

"His dry-cleaning place is on the news right now. It's burning to the fucking ground."

I looked up at him.

"My dad just left the city and now L.A. is on fire?"

"Damn."

"Damn, is right, Sam. Let's go."

Dominick's Mercedes slowly entered the alley behind Rose's Liquor. Salvatore exited the back door carrying a black duffel bag with Carmine following behind. Both Corso brothers climbed into the backseat.

We arrived in the industrial section of Los Angeles later that night. There was nothing but tall bleak factories and warehouses. Yet, a very stylish bar was hidden in the area called The Lounge.

Dominick opened the trunk. He unzipped the black duffel bag and held it open wide enough so that we all could see inside.

"Know what these are, Sam?"

"Grenades!?" My voice echoed all the way down the street.

Rudy laughed.

"Look." He removed one from the bag. "This is the lever, and this is the primer. It's simple. Here."

It was heavy in my hand like an expensive toy and without

warning, Dominick removed the small pin.

I tried to force it back into his hands.

"Relax. As long as you hold the lever, it won't blow up. See." Dominick stuck the pin into its proper place and I finally released the lever.

Rudy: "This is what we're gonna' do, Sammy boy. Hold down the lever, take the pin out, let go of the lever for about ten seconds, then throw it inside the bar."

I pointed. "That bar right there?"

Carmine: "You see any other bars around here?"

Dominick gave us all ski masks and two grenades each.

"The guys that tried to kidnap my sister own that bar." Dominick said. "And do you know the fastest way to hurt somebody?"

"Throw grenades at him." Salvatore answered, causing Carmine and Rudy to laugh.

After the masks were on, we began walking towards the bar. Rudy walked ahead of us and took out the infamous golden handgun. Pointing it towards the sky, he fired three shots.

BOOM! BOOM! BOOM!

The people standing in the doorway of the bar dropped to the ground before scattering away.

And there we were, the five of us standing 10 feet from the entrance of The Lounge with grenades in our pockets and the moon behind us.

Dominick tossed his grenade first and it exploded when it touched the wooden floorboard inside the bar.

He looked at me. "For my sister."

I removed a grenade from my pocket, pulled the pin out, and threw it. I heard the **knock** as it hit the polished floor and after, there was nothing except blinding light and metal fragments.

Dominick nodded his head in approval.

Into my nostrils travelled the scent of overcooked meat. I heard guns being fired by blinded men.

"Bombs away!" Rudy yelled, throwing one of his grenades

inside the bar.

Salvatore and Carmine removed the pins from their grenades and tossed them inside the bar.

There was finally a silence to everything until Rudy yelled,

"At the same time!"

Five more grenades landed inside The Lounge.

In the end, the place looked as if an angry giant had chewed a large portion of the bar and then vomited it back up.

Dominick calmly turned his back on the destroyed building. "Let's go."

Rudy: "Ride with me, Sam."

I watched as the Corso brothers climbed into Dominick's Mercedes and disappeared.

Rudy started the engine of his Porsche as we removed our masks and wiped our sweaty faces with them.

"You did good today. And you did good the other day too." Rudy reached into the backseat to retrieve a white envelope. "This is yours."

Inside was a thick stack of cash.

"This is your cut, Sammy boy."

"For what?"

"Boss said to give you this."

"Damn. Thanks."

"Don't thank me. Thank Mr. Morello next time you see him."

Then, Rudy slid his sunglasses on smoothly before glancing at a confident reflection in the rearview mirror.

CHAPTER FOURTEEN

I was awakened at three in the morning by three loud knocks on my door. I opened it.

"Philly!"

"Yo!"

"Bro! Where the hell have you been!?"

He walked inside.

"I went to Mexico with this one chick." He began. "It was only supposed to be for the weekend, right? Everything got fucked up. We damn near had to sneak back over the border. I'm just now getting back to L.A."

"What?"

"It's a long story, Sam. So, what's been up? Did you publish that book yet?"

Some sense of normalcy returned for the both of us as we drank beers and smoked together. I gave him a brief summary of what happened since he'd been away and any time I paused in the story, he shouted,

"I want in!"

There was a harsh knock at the door.

Knock.

I walked towards the sound and when I was almost there, the wooden door swung open hitting me in the face.

A flash of light filled my eyes and I fell. Four people entered my apartment and while I was on the floor, they began kicking me viciously.

During the beating, Phil grabbed a gun.

"Get the fuck off my friend!"

He squeezed the trigger and shot one of them in the stomach. The man dropped and screamed.

The other three pointed their handguns at Phil.

Boom! Boom! Boom! Boom! Boom! Boom! Boom! Boom!

The shots shook my apartment as Philly ducked behind my couch. The warm shells continued raining on top of me. Phil kept firing wildly. One man fell next to me after a stray bullet hit him in the neck.

I grabbed his gun and then lifted my eyes just in time to witness my best friend get shot.

He blinked slowly at me, and

without trying to soften the impact, he fell face first. His head slammed against the wooden floor.

One of the men walked over to Phil and flipped him over unto his back.

I could hear my friend faintly breathing.

That's when I raised the gun and shot the guy standing over me three times in the chest.

"Phil!" I yelled, pointing the gun at the man standing over my friend.

I pulled the trigger and the man fell dead.

I looked around at all the bodies lying in my apartment and all of a sudden, my eyes went blurry and I blacked-out.

*****

I opened my eyes, expecting to either be in Heaven or in a hospital emergency room. Instead, I woke up face down on my living room floor. All the bodies were still lying stiff, including Philly.

I called out to him in a whisper. He didn't move. I forced myself up and there was pool of blood around him and a dark red stain on the front of his shirt. I shook him hard, and he opened his eyes and began moaning.

"Phil!" I yelled. "Phil! Wake up! C'mon, man!"

"What!? What the fuck happened, Sam!?"

"Some guys busted in here. They tried to kill us."

"What?"

I helped him up and sat him on the couch.

I found my phone underneath the couch with a hundred missed calls from Maria, but the first person I called was Louie. He arrived in less than 10 minutes with the Corso brothers. They entered my apartment with their guns out.

"Ouch!" Louie said, looking at my face. "They beat the shit outta you, Sammy. Damn."

And then they all looked at Phil on the couch, and Salvatore pointed his gun at him and said,

"Who the fuck is this?"

"Woah," I began. "This is my

friend Phil. He got shot. He needs help bad."

"Phil?" Louie asked. "Oh yeah. The driver."

"The driver?" Philly asked."

"You drove me to the liquor store when I robbed it. So that's what they call you: The Driver."

"Well can somebody please take me to the fucking hospital?"

"What are you nuts or something?" Carmine asked. "Doctors tell cops when people walk in with gunshot wounds. Can't have that."

"Don't worry, kid." Louie said, walking over to Phil.

He looked at where he got shot.

"Fuck. The bullet is still in your shoulder. But, we got a guy that can help you. He'll clean you up and you'll be as right as rain."

"Thanks."

I walked to the bathroom and stuck tissue into my nostrils to slow the bleeding. I lifted my shirt and saw the blues and purples that illuminated the sides of my stomach. I felt like I had been hit by a bus.

"Get what you need, Sam."
Louie yelled. "We gotta get the
fuck out of here."

Inside my backpack, I only
took some clothes, the envelope
with money in it, and a gun.

As we exited my apartment, one
of the attackers began stirring
awake in pain on the floor. We all
stopped as Carmine walked over to
him.

He put the barrel of his gun
in the guy's bloody mouth and
asked,

"Are you praying? Last words?
No? You know, I can't understand
you, man. Well, I tried."

BOOM!

Carmine killed him.

CHAPTER FIFTEEN

As we drove away from my apartment, there was a single **THUMP** against Louie's car. With no hesitation, Louie leaned over, opened the glove compartment, and removed a .357 revolver.

"Keep your head down, guys." He told Philly and me.

I looked into the passenger mirror and saw two BMW's almost touching our bumper. Both cars switched to opposite lanes and ended up on either side of us.

As Louie accelerated around some cars, the back window shattered.

Louie stuck his .357 out and fired at the BMW to our left. I watched it swerve into head on traffic.

Before I could pull the trigger at the BMW on my side, it veered to the left smashing into us and I dropped my gun on the floorboard. By the time I picked it up, the driver was pointing a sub-machine gun at my face.

"Oh shit!" Philly screamed. "Sam! Watch out!"

I'm done, I thought, until he

collided hard into a parked truck.
CRASH!

I glanced to my left and Louie was bleeding from the shoulder while steadily dodging traffic.

I jumped into the backseat with Philly and began shooting while bullets screamed back at me.

Louie pulled the emergency brake, and the sudden stop threw me and Phil to the floor. By the time I rose, the other car passed and had turned around to face us.

"Seatbelts! Now!"

Louie mashed the gas pedal. Phil and I watched from the backseat as we sped towards the BMW at full speed.

On impact, my whole body jerked forward, and I slammed my head against the front headrest.

I lost consciousness until I heard the driver side car door open.

Amidst the wreckage, Louie stepped out and I watched him shoot into all four BMW windows.

* * * * *

At the University, I snuck

past the security guard at the entrance and went straight to Maria's dorm room. She opened the door and pulled me right in.

CHAPTER SIXTEEN

My ringing phone woke me up. It was Rudy.

"Sam. I heard what happened last night. It's a good thing you made it out alive. Our doctor got the bullet out of your friend Phil's arm. He's getting stitched up right now. And I know who sent those guys to your apartment to kill you. Meet me at Rose's Liquor Store in 10 minutes."

END.

I looked over at Maria.

"Please don't go," she said. "Just stay here with me. Please."

"I have to go."

I drove away torn between love and revenge. The latter won, and there I was parking in the alley behind Rudy's Porsche. He exited the backdoor of Rose's Liquor Store with a large duffel bag as I leaned against a graffitied wall. He rested his hand on my shoulder before removing a joint from his breast pocket. He handed it to me. Once I lit it, he said,

"Damn, you sure did get your

ass whooped, Sam. But I got a present for you."

"A present?"

"Yep. I know the son of a bitch who sent those guys to your place. And I know where he's at right now."

"How'd he find out where I live?"

"Who the fuck knows, Sammy boy. Those fuckers are our enemies. That's how. But you're with the Morello Crime Family. And nobody fucks with a guy on our crew. Nobody. So we need to show people what happens when they fuck with us."

"Where is the guy?"

"The Hotel."

"Who is he?"

"He's the heir of our rival's crew. If we clip his ass, it'll put a dent in their whole organization. He owns a suite on the top floor of The Hotel and he's throwing a party tonight. Let's go."

* * * * *

Rudy and I arrived at The

Hotel that night. The girl working behind the desk winked at him and then gave him a card key.

Once we made it to our room, Rudy unzipped the black bag, and removed two bullet proof vests, two ski masks, and two machine guns.

"What the hell is that?"

"That," he said, "is a Tommy gun. Al Capone. Bonnie & Clyde type shit. 45 round magazine. We could sweep a whole damn street with these."

His phone rang, and once the call ended, he nodded his head at me and said,

"It's time."

We pulled the ski masks over our heads and strapped the heavy bulletproof vests across our chests and exited the room.

In the hallway was a woman. She was standing there in a very tight form fitting red dress. Her heels looked sharp enough to cut a man's throat. Ashes landed on the overpriced carpet as she smoked a cigarette.

"Rudy, my love." She rubbed her hands on his ski mask. "The

man you were asking about, he's in there. There's three other men with them and they all have guns. They're halfway drunk and having fun with my girls."

"Your money is in our room inside the black bag." Rudy told her.

"Don't hurt my girls in there."

She disappeared into our room, and I asked Rudy,

"Who is she?"

"She's a killer, Sammy boy. A Russian killer. You ready or what?"

"I'm ready."

He punched me in the chest. "Well, look ready then, motherfucker."

Sandy left the door to Ken's suite open so we wouldn't need a room key.

There was loud music blaring from speakers and Rudy and I both stood in the doorway for without anyone looking in our direction except the dancing girls. They knew what was coming. So, while the men's eyes were glued to the half-naked women, they were oblivious that two men in ski masks were blocking their only exit with automatic guns.

Rudy and I took a step inside.

One of the bedroom doors opened and out walked a naked guy. Two naked girls followed. One of them tripped on a Jim Beam whiskey bottle and fell to the floor pulling the other down.

"That's him." Rudy said, and without warning, he raised his Tommy Gun and began shooting.

The girls screamed and ducked to the floor.

The naked man jumped behind a white couch as bullets tore through it.

Rudy then shot the three bodyguards. I remember the barrel tip of his gun was glowing red.

"Yeah, motherfucker's! Yeah!" Rudy screamed, as round after round spun from his gun.

When the noise stopped, all the girls ran past us out of the hotel room.

Rudy and I stepped over the three dead bodyguards. The guy behind the white couch was crawling away from Rudy and I towards one of the bedrooms; a trail of his blood following him.

Rudy kicked his legs and he flipped over.

"Nobody messes with the Morello Crime Family," Rudy said.

The man looked at both of us and gave us the finger.

"Go to hell," he responded calmly.

Rudy shrugged and then shot him to death.

He then looked at me and said, "Shoot that big window out."

After I did so, Rudy dragged the guy over.

"Help me, Sam. We're throwing him out. All the other crews will get the message from now on: stay-the-fuck-away-from-L.A."

We watched the body fall from the top floor and crash violently into the sidewalk.

CHAPTER SEVENTEEN

I didn't recognize Morello's Italian Cuisine at all.

News helicopters circled above while fire fighters pumped tons of water at what was only burned debris.

I exited my car and hurried past police officers who were sealing off the area with red tape.

I saw Rudy sitting on the ground next to his Porsche. Louie, Dominick, Salvatore, and Carmine were all crowded around him.

"What happened!?"

"They got us good, Sam" Louie answered. "They burned the whole place down."

"What the fuck." I whispered.

"Benny and Dimples are gone."

"Gone?"

"Yeah. Gone."

I bent down next to Rudy and put my hand on his shoulder. When he looked up at me, all I saw was anger.

"What's the next move, Dominick?" Salvatore asked.

When Rudy rose from the

ground, Dominick helped him wipe tears from his face.

"It's time to end this." Dominick said. "I'm tired of playing with these fucks. What else do we know about their crew?"

"There's a hair salon on the other side of town." Louie said. "Rumor is, it's a front for laundering all their crew's dirty money. Let's go there."

"Sam, you ride with me." Rudy said.

I got into the Porsche. Dominick, Louie, and the Corso brothers climbed into a Benz.

"Rudy…I'm sorry about your dad." I said, as he sped out of the parking lot.

We parked across the street from the hair salon and before Dominick and the others arrived, Rudy had already stuck four pistols into his waistband.

After handing me one, he asked,

"Ready?"

"Yeah. But, don't we need ski masks?"

He didn't answer and began walking across the street,

ignoring all the cars honking and swerving around us.

Rudy opened fire towards the hair salon.

As he stepped over dying men, they got a bullet in the head each.

Dominick, Louie, and the Corso brothers arrived just before Rudy entered the hair salon shooting anything that moved with zero mercy. And when one of his guns ran out of bullets, he simply dropped it and grabbed another like a stick of gum that had lost its flavor.

That's when a separate car full of enemies entered the scene and guys exited with automatic weapons blazing towards us.

Louie, Dominick, Sal, and Carmine returned fire at them.

Rudy ignored it all, continuing to kick a door leading to a back room. I watched him shoot the handle and then kick the door open. He entered and returned, savagely dragging a woman by the hair to the middle of the salon. She desperately fought, trying to escape his grip. Rudy pushed her to the floor and pointed both guns at her.

"Fuck you!" She screamed. "Do you know who the fuck I am!?"

Rudy shot her right in the face.

Another carload of armed men showed up.

Louie dropped when a bullet flew straight through his eye.

Dominick was reloading his gun when I saw three bullets burn through his stomach.

I hid behind a wall as hot lead seared past me.

I peeked out only to witness Salvatore take a bullet to the chest. When Carmine dropped down to help his brother, he got shot in his head.

I was trapped.

I looked up at the ceiling and realized that I was next. I thought of Maria. She was alone and I wouldn't be around to protect her.

BOOM! BOOM! BOOM! BOOM! BOOM! BOOM!

Silence.

"Sam! Sam! Over here!"

I looked and Rudy was outside

the hair salon ducking behind a car. I ran towards him and he threw me his car keys. I zigzagged through a maze of cars and scared citizens towards his Porsche as bullets followed us. Rudy continued firing while moving backwards until he reached the passenger side of his car.

"The freeway, Sam! Go!"

Before we entered the on-ramp, a bullet flew through the back window and continued out the front.

"Drive, Sam! Drive!"

Rudy stuck half of his body out of the window and began shooting at the trailing car.

BOOM! BOOM! BOOM! BOOM! BOOM! BOOM!

"Fuck." He whispered, sitting back into the seat.

I glanced over and Rudy was bleeding from the shoulder.

"Son of a fucking bitch!" He yelled, reaching into the backseat to grab a fully automatic assault rifle.

Rudy: "Slow down, Sam."

I gently raised my foot off the gas pedal, and I watched the

BMW quickly close the gap in the rearview mirror. When it was the distance of a car away, Rudy popped out of the window with the AR-15 and ripped the front of the BMW to pieces.

When he sat back in his seat, Rudy was gripping his neck. Dark red blood raced down his fingers.

"Rudy!"

I heard the gurgling of blood in his throat and all I could do was yell his name repeatedly.

"Rudy!"

Burning tears blurred my vision as I sped towards the hospital.

When I stopped at the hospital's emergency entrance, I carefully slid Rudy's limp body out.

"Help!" I screamed. "Please! Somebody help!"

Two nurses ran from behind their desk over to me.

"Doctor!" One of them yelled.

I watched them take Rudy past the swinging doors on a stretcher and I knew it would be the last time I'd ever see him again.

I returned to Maria's dorm room and she immediately stuffed her backpack with clothes.

I called Philly.

"Hey, bro. Maria and me are leaving L.A. You need to come with us."

"Fuck that. I'm not running anywhere."

"Those guys won't stop until we're all dead, Philly."

Silence.

"Well, I got my gun on me too." He responded. "So they can fuck off."

We laughed.

"Where are you going, Sam?"

"Mexico."

"Mexico?"

"Yeah."

"Nice. Bring me back some firecrackers."

"I'm not coming back."

"My best friend in the whole world is going to Mexico and he won't even bring me back some firecrackers? I got shot protecting your ass. What is this world coming to?"

We laughed.

"Check this out." Phil began. "I went back to your apartment. It's officially a crime scene. Yellow tape everywhere. Chalk lines on the floor. But I snuck in and grabbed all your notebooks. I got all your stories, bro! I'll publish the book here. Be safe in Mexico."

"Damn, Philly. Thanks, man."

"I'll see you when you get back, Sam. Peace."

But I was certain that I'd never ever see L.A. ever again.

* * * * *

Inside my BMW, Maria and I had one backpack each filled with clothes.

And for hours, we sped towards the southern border into the morning.

-The End